GARFIELD EXTREME CUISINE PIGGING WAY OUT!

Created by
JIM DAVIS

Written by Scott Nickel
Designed and illustrated by Mike Fentz

Troll

This edition published in 2002 by Troll Communications L.L.C.
All rights reserved. No part of this book may be reproduced or utilized in any form or by
any means, electronic or mechanical, including photocopying, recording, or by any
information storage and retrieval system, without written permission from the publisher.
ISBN 0-8167-7432-3   Printed in the United States of America.
10 9 8 7 6 5 4 3 2 1

One lazy Sunday afternoon, Garfield, Odie, and Jon were lounging on the sofa watching TV.

"These extreme sports are incredible!" declared Jon, pointing to the screen. "Sky surfing, mountain biking, bungee jumping . . . I'll bet *you* could never do anything like that, Garfield!"

The tubby tabby scowled. "I'll bet I'd never *want* to do anything like that," he muttered. "All they're doing is burning calories. I like activities where I can *consume* calories!"

"Arf!" Odie seconded.

"Hey, wait a minute!" Garfield's face brightened. "This gives me a great idea. Let's go, Odie!"

Grabbing the perplexed pooch, Garfield raced out the door and into Jon's garage, where he pulled some strange-looking items out of a cardboard box.

"Here, Odie, put these on," Garfield instructed.

"Huh?" questioned Odie.

Moments later, the fat cat and the drooling dog emerged from the garage dressed to kill—or at least maim—in crash helmets, gloves, and elbow, knee, and shoulder pads.

"We'll show that dweeby Jon," Garfield said. "Now we're ready for our *own* extreme sports—some games we can *really* sink our teeth into!"

Odie gave his feline friend a puzzled look but obediently followed him down the street.

KABOOM! Garfield and Odie burst through the doors of Le Grand Gourmet, the fanciest restaurant in town.

"Banzai!" cried Garfield. "Let the games begin!"

The tubby tabby leaped onto a table in the middle of the crowded restaurant, sending the well-dressed diners running for cover.

"First, an appetizer," Garfield said, grinning. "Let's start with a game of 'Breadstick Billiards.'" He picked up a long breadstick and aimed it at a plate of Swedish meatballs.

"Meatball in the corner pocket," announced the fat cat, using the breadstick as a pool cue and hitting the meaty morsels—SMACK! Meatballs flew through the air. A large one bounced off the far wall of the restaurant, ricocheted off a serving cart, and landed right in Garfield's mouth.

The frightened customers of Le Grand Gourmet hid under their tables, watching the food fly. Pierre, the restaurant's tuxedoed maitre d', rushed over to Garfield and Odie, madly waving his arms.

"Stop! Stop!" Pierre shouted. "You crazy creatures will ruin my restaurant! Besides, you don't even have a reservation!"

"Chill out," said Garfield, "or you won't get a good tip when we leave." He sprinkled some pepper in his paw and blew it at the angry maitre d'.

"Achoo! Achoo!" Pierre sneezed hard, stumbled backward, and sat down in a bowl of hot onion soup. "Yeowch!"

"Now that he's out of the way, on to our next event," said Garfield. "Odie, how about a little 'Biscuitball' action?" Garfield jumped onto another table and grabbed a large round biscuit. "It's you and me, one-on-one—or in this case, one-on-dumb!" the feline taunted.

Garfield tossed the biscuit to Odie, who, much to the cat's surprise, caught it in his mouth and began bouncing it with his tongue.

"I knew you could drool, Odie, but I didn't know you could dribble!" said Garfield.

But Odie's hoop dreams were swiftly shattered, as the feisty feline slapped the biscuit from Odie's tongue and began dribbling down the long table.

"You're no match for Doctor G!" declared Garfield, breaking into a play-by-play description of the action.

"Garfield gets the biscuit . . . he fakes left, then right, he shoots . . . he scores! And the crowd goes wild!" the cat exclaimed, as the biscuit splashed into a large gravy server. Garfield then picked up the gravy-soaked morsel and jammed it into his mouth. "Gulp! Now *that's* what I call stuffing the ball! Score's 2-0!"

Odie let out a bone-rattling growl, picked up a fork between his teeth, and jumped to another table, ready to pounce on a thick filet mignon steak.

"So you want to play a little 'Meat Hockey' now?" asked Garfield, picking up his own fork and advancing toward the steak.

Using the fork like a hockey stick, Garfield slid the filet off its plate and tossed it onto the slick waxed floor. Then he and Odie jumped down and stood nose-to-nose over the beefy "puck."

"It's the face-off, fleabag!" the "Great Garfsky" grunted, scooping up the steak with his makeshift hockey stick and gliding it across the floor.

Without warning, Odie swung by with his fork, swiped the steak away from the cat, and quickly maneuvered it in the opposite direction. Skidding to a stop, Odie took aim, and with a loud thwack, sent the filet mignon hurtling through the air.

Garfield ran as fast as his tubby legs would carry him past the flying filet, turned, and with a loud "Gulp!" caught it in his mouth.

"Another point for me!" Garfield said proudly.

"Grr!" Odie grumbled.

"That's enough out of you four-legged furballs," the furious maitre d' cried, running toward Garfield and Odie with a large net. "Someone call the police!" Pierre wailed. "Call the fire department! Call the pound!"

"Uh-oh," said Garfield. "Looks like we're going to have to eat and run!"

The fat orange cat and the dopey dog hopped onto a serving cart and rolled quickly away, with Pierre in hot pursuit. As the terrible twosome careened from table to table, they swiped samples of the fancy food.

"Hey, Pierre!" shouted Garfield. "The gravy is a little runny at table six!"

But Garfield's wild ride was cut short as he and Odie rounded a table and collided head-on with a large metal salad bowl that had landed on the floor during the action.

KA-TONG! The force of the impact sent the salad sailing, and Garfield and Odie tumbled head-over-wheels onto the floor and out the doorway.

"Talk about a tossed salad," Garfield said, wiping the gooey romaine lettuce and cherry tomatoes off his face and arms.

At that moment, Pierre appeared. "Good-bye and good riddance!" he yelled, slamming the doors closed.

"Looks as if we're shut out," Garfield said. "And speaking of shutouts, Odie, you remain scoreless, not to mention clueless."

Odie looked at Garfield and whimpered.

"But it's not over yet . . ." the fat cat said with a sly grin.

KABOOM! Garfield and Odie burst through the doors of Le Grand Goodies, the fanciest bakery in town.

"Banzai!" cried Garfield. "Now it's time for extreme *dessert!!*"